THIS WALKER BOOK BELONGS TO:

_____

_____

_____

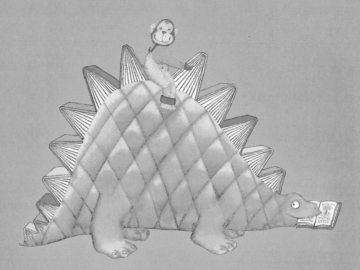

First published 1988 by Julia MacRae Books
This edition published 2003 by Walker Books Ltd
87 Vauxhall Walk, London SE11 5HJ

11 13 15 17 19 20 18 16 14 12

This book has been typeset in Melior Educational

Printed in China

British Library Cataloguing in Publication Data:
a catalogue record for this book is available from the British Library

ISBN 978-0-7445-9857-5

www.walker.co.uk

I Like Books

ANTHONY BROWNE

WALKER BOOKS
AND SUBSIDIARIES

LONDON · BOSTON · SYDNEY · AUCKLAND

I like books.

Funny books ...

and scary books.

Fairy tales ...

and nursery rhymes.

Comic books ...

and colouring books.

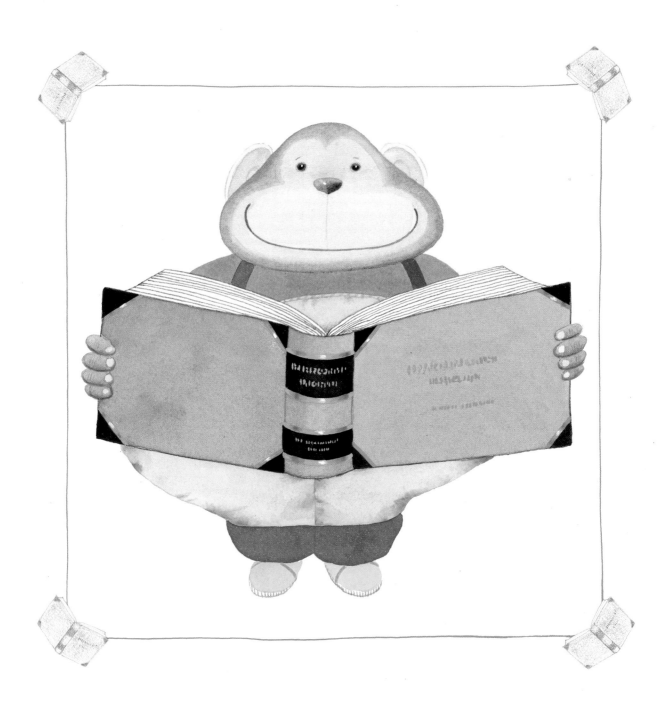

Fat books ...

and thin books.

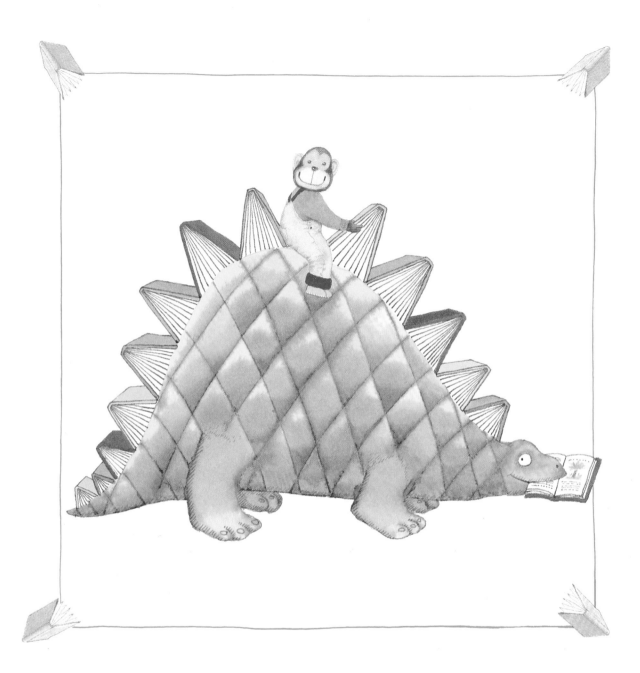

Books about dinosaurs ...

and books about monsters.

Counting books ...

and alphabet books.

Books about space ...

and books about pirates.

Song books ...

and strange books.

Yes, I really do like books.

WALKER BOOKS BY ANTHONY BROWNE

★ WILLY'S PICTURES
HIGHLY COMMENDED FOR THE KATE GREENAWAY MEDAL

★ GORILLA
WINNER OF THE KATE GREENAWAY MEDAL

WILLY THE WIMP

WILLY THE CHAMP

WILLY THE DREAMER

HANSEL AND GRETEL

SILLY BILLY

PLAY THE SHAPE GAME

THROUGH THE MAGIC MIRROR

THINGS I LIKE • I LIKE BOOKS

CHANGES • THE TUNNEL

LOOK WHAT I'VE GOT!

PIGGYBOOK

THE ANIMAL FAIR

INTO THE FOREST

LITTLE BEAUTY

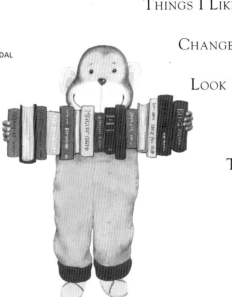

AVAILABLE FROM ALL GOOD BOOKSTORES

www.walker.co.uk